THE BIGGEST BOY

BY KEVIN HENKES
ILLUSTRATED BY NANCY TAFURI

GREENWILLOW BOOKS · NEW YORK

For Laura
—K. H.

For Cristina
—N. T.

Watercolor inks and a black pen
were used for the full-color art.
The text type is Americana.

Printed in Singapore by
Tien Wah Press

First Edition 10 9 8 7 6 5 4 3 2 1

Library of Congress
Cataloging-in-Publication Data

Henkes, Kevin.
The biggest boy / by Kevin Henkes;
pictures by Nancy Tafuri.
       p.   cm.
Summary: Billy and his parents
discuss how big he is getting.
ISBN 0-688-12829-7 (trade).
ISBN 0-688-12830-0 (lib. bdg.)
[1. Size—Fiction.]
I. Tafuri, Nancy, ill.   II. Title.
PZ7.H389Bi   1995   [E]—dc20
94-4574   CIP   AC

This is Billy.

He is a big boy.
He can eat with a fork.
He can get dressed all alone.
And he can even reach some of
the cupboards in the kitchen.

Billy can put his boots on by himself (and snap them!).
He can answer the telephone.
And he can even help
with the dishes.

"You are growing every day,"
  says his mother.
"Bigger and bigger and bigger,"
  says his father.
"Soon we'll have to buy you
  new pants," says his mother.
"And new shoes," says his father.
"I'll even be bigger than that,"
  says Billy.

"Soon you'll go to school,"
    says his mother.
"Soon you'll ride a bike,"
    says his father.
"Bigger," says Billy.
"How big?" says his mother.
"How big?" says his father.
"So big," says Billy, "I'll even
    be bigger than you. I'll be the
    biggest boy in the world."

"If you are the biggest boy," says his mother, "then you can wear the roof as a hat."
"You can stick your arms out the windows," says his father. "The house can be your jacket. Dogs and cats can live in your pockets."
Billy giggles. "That's big!" he says.

"You won't have to fly to Grammy's," says his mother. "You can walk there in two steps."

"You will have to drink from the lakes," says his father. "And eat forty apples for a snack."

Billy giggles again. "Big!" he says.

"You can move the clouds by blowing on them," says his mother.

"You can hang a rainbow
around your neck," says his father.
Billy laughs and laughs.

"You will be so big,"
says his mother,
"you can toss the
sun up like a ball
and catch it."

"And when the moon is thin and curvy," says his father, "you can wear it as a mustache." Billy laughs and laughs and laughs some more.

"But right now,"
  says his mother,
"you are just the
  right size for a big
  boy your age."
"Just right,"
  says his father.

"And right now it's bedtime
for a big boy your age,"
says his mother.
"Exactly," says his father.
Billy is such a big boy,
he climbs into bed by himself
and gets comfortable.

After one kiss and more kisses
and saying good night,

Billy stares at the moon.
He holds his hand up to it,
and the moon is no bigger
than a marble.
"I really am the biggest boy,"
says Billy.

And in his dreams he <u>is</u>.